THE BEE-MAN
OF ORN

for Daddy and Ben

P.J.L.

Frank R. Stockton
The Bee-man of Orn

ILLUSTRATED BY
P.J. Lynch

WALKER BOOKS
AND SUBSIDIARIES
LONDON • BOSTON • SYDNEY • AUCKLAND

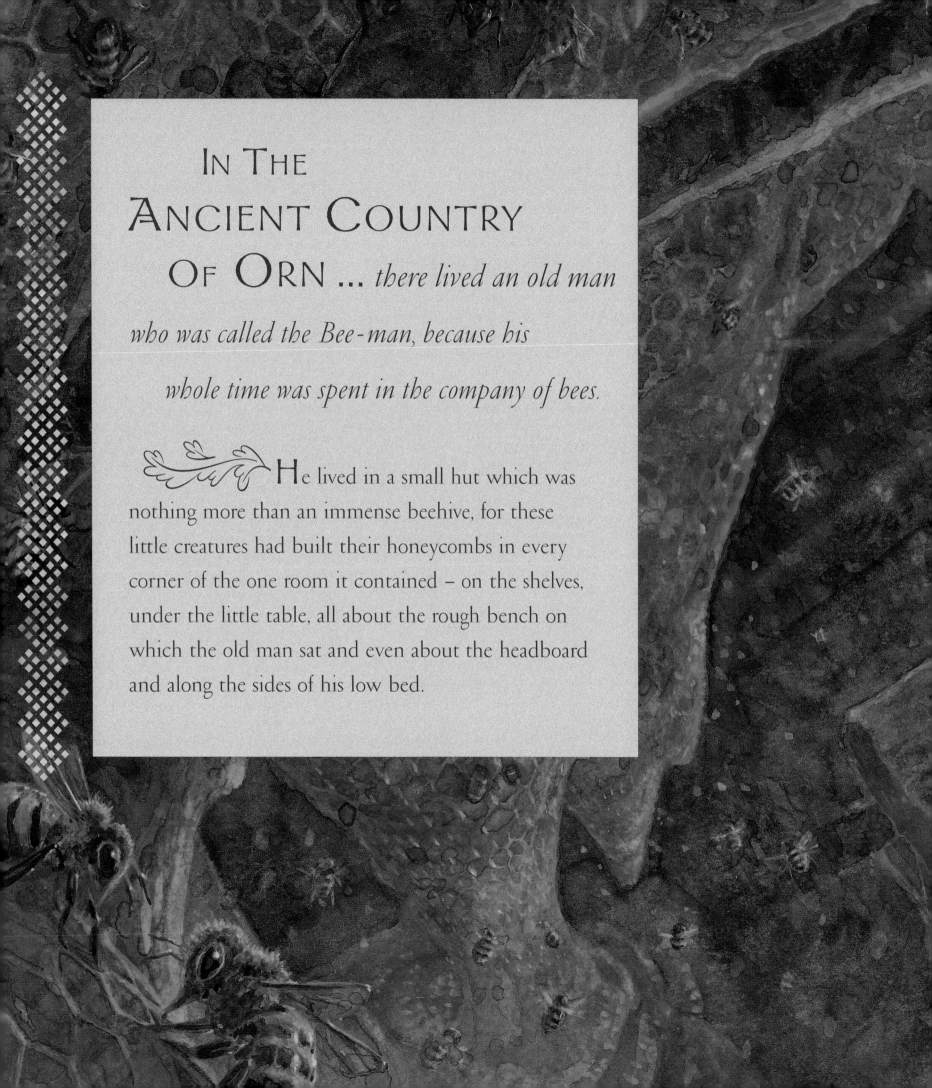

IN THE ANCIENT COUNTRY OF ORN ... *there lived an old man*

who was called the Bee-man, because his

whole time was spent in the company of bees.

He lived in a small hut which was nothing more than an immense beehive, for these little creatures had built their honeycombs in every corner of the one room it contained – on the shelves, under the little table, all about the rough bench on which the old man sat and even about the headboard and along the sides of his low bed.

All day the air of the room was thick with buzzing insects, but this did not interfere in any way with the old Bee-man, who walked in among them, ate his meals and went to sleep without the slightest fear of being stung. He had lived with the bees so long, they had become so accustomed to him and his skin was so tough and hard that they no more thought of stinging him than they would of stinging a tree or a stone.

A swarm of bees made their hive in a pocket of his old leather doublet; and when he put on this coat to take one of his long walks in the forest in search of wild bees' nests, he was very glad to have this hive with him, for if he did not find any wild honey he would put his hand in his pocket and take out a piece of honeycomb for a luncheon. The bees in his pocket worked very industriously, and he was always certain of having something to eat with him wherever he went. He lived principally upon honey, and when he needed bread or meat he carried some fine combs to a village near by and bartered them for other food. He was ugly, untidy, shrivelled and sunburnt. He was poor, and the bees seemed to be his only friends.

But, for all that, he was happy and contented. He had all the honey he wanted, and his bees, whom he considered the best company in the world, were as friendly and sociable as they could be, and seemed to increase in number every day.

One day there stopped at the hut of the Bee-man a Junior Sorcerer. This young person, who was a student of magic, necromancy and the kindred arts, was much interested in the Bee-man, whom he had frequently noticed in his wanderings, and he considered him an admirable subject for study. He had had a great deal of useful practice in endeavouring to find out, by the various rules and laws of sorcery, exactly why the old Bee-man did not happen to be something that he was not, and why he was what he happened to be. He had studied this matter a long time, and had found out something.

"Do you know," he said when the Bee-man came out of his hut, "that you have been transformed?"

"What do you mean by that?" said the other, much surprised. "You have surely heard of animals and human beings who have been magically transformed into different kinds of creatures?"

"Yes, I have heard of these things," said the Bee-man. "But what have I been transformed from?"

"That is more than I know," said the Junior Sorcerer. "But one thing is certain – you ought to be changed back. If you will find out what you have been transformed from, I will see that you are made all right again. Nothing would please me better than to attend to such a case."

Then, having a great many things to study and investigate, the Junior Sorcerer went his way.

This information greatly disturbed the mind of the Bee-man. If he had been changed from something else, he ought to be that other thing, whatever it was. He ran after the young man, and overtook him.

"If you know, kind sir," he said, "that I have been transformed, you surely are able to tell me what it is that I was."

"No," said the Junior Sorcerer, "my studies have not proceeded far enough for that. When I become a senior I can tell you all about it. But in the meantime it will be well for you to try to discover for yourself your original form; and when you have done that, I will get some of the learned masters of my art to restore you to it. It will be easy enough to do that, but you cannot expect them to take the time and trouble to find out what it was."

With these words, he hurried away and was soon lost to view.

Greatly disquieted, the Bee-man retraced his steps and went to his hut. Never before had he heard anything which had so troubled him.

I wonder what I was transformed from? he thought, seating himself on his rough bench. Could it have been a giant, or a powerful prince, or some gorgeous being whom the magicians or the fairies wished to punish? It may be that I was a dog or a horse, or perhaps a fiery dragon or a horrid snake. I hope it was not one of these. But whatever it was, everyone has certainly a right to his original form, and I am resolved to find out mine. I will start early tomorrow morning, and I am sorry now I have not more pockets to my old doublet, so that I might carry more bees and more honey for my journey.

He spent the rest of the day in
making a hive of twigs and straw,
and when he had transferred to this
some honeycombs and a colony of
bees which had just swarmed, he rose
before sunrise the next day, put on his
leather doublet, bound his new hive
to his back and set forth on his quest,
the bees who were to accompany him
buzzing about him like a cloud.

As the Bee-man passed through the little village, the people greatly wondered at his queer appearance, with the hive upon his back. "The Bee-man is going on a long expedition this time," they said. But no one imagined the strange business on which he was bent. About noon he sat down under a tree, near a beautiful meadow covered with blossoms and ate a little honey.

Then he untied his hive and stretched himself out on the grass to rest. As he gazed upon his bees hovering above him, some going out to the blossoms in the sunshine and some returning laden with the sweet pollen, he said to himself, "They know just what they have to do, and they do it. But alas for me! I know not what I may have to do. And yet, whatever it may be, I am determined to do it. In

UWE Library Services

Frenchay Campus
Tel: 0117 32 82277

Borrowed Items 17/11/2015 23:11
XXXX7066

Item Title	Due Date
The Bee-Man of Orn	16/03/2016 23:59

Please note items are subject to recall at
at any time. Please check your UWE
email regularly for notifications.
www.uwe.ac.uk/library

some way or other I will find out what was my original form, and then I will have myself changed back to it."

And now the thought again came to him that perhaps his original form might have been something very disagreeable, or even horrid. "But it does not matter," he said sturdily. "Whatever I was, that shall I be again. It is not right for anyone to retain a form which does not properly belong to him. I have no doubt I shall discover my original form in the same way that I find the trees in which the wild bees hive. When I first catch sight of a bee tree I am drawn towards it, I know not how. Something says to me, 'That is what you are looking for.' In the same way I believe that I shall find my original form. When I see it, I shall be drawn towards it. Something will say to me, 'That is it.'"

When the Bee-man had rested he started off again, and in about an hour he entered a fair domain. Around him were beautiful lawns, grand trees and lovely gardens, while at a little distance stood the stately palace of the Lord of the Domain. Richly dressed people were walking about or sitting in the shade of the trees and arbors, splendidly caparisoned horses were waiting for their riders and everywhere were seen signs of opulence and gaiety.

"I think," said the Bee-man to himself, "that I should like to stop here for a time. If it should happen that I was originally like any of these happy creatures it would please me much."

He untied his hive and hid it behind some bushes, and taking off his old doublet, laid that beside it. It would not do to have his bees flying about him if he wished to go among the inhabitants of this fair domain.

For two days the Bee-man wandered about the palace and its grounds, avoiding notice as much as possible but looking at everything. He saw handsome men and lovely ladies, the finest horses, dogs and cattle that were ever known, beautiful birds in cages and fishes in crystal globes, and it seemed to him that the best of all living things were here collected.

At the close of the second day the Bee-man said to himself, "There is one being here towards whom I feel very much drawn, and that is the Lord of the Domain. I cannot feel certain that I was once like him, but it would be a very fine thing if it were so; and it seems impossible for me to be drawn towards any other being in the domain when I look upon him, so handsome, rich and powerful. But I must observe him more closely, and feel more sure of the matter, before applying to the sorcerers to change me back into a lord of a fair domain."

The next morning the Bee-man saw the Lord of the Domain walking in his gardens. He slipped along the shady paths and followed him, so as to observe him closely and find out if he were really drawn towards this noble and handsome being. The Lord of the Domain walked on for some time, not noticing that the Bee-man was behind him. But suddenly turning, he saw the little old man.

"What are you doing here, you vile beggar?" he cried, and he gave him a kick that sent him into some bushes that grew by the side of the path.

The Bee-man scrambled to his feet and ran as fast as he could to the place where he had hidden his hive and his old doublet. If I am certain of anything, he thought, it is that I was never a person who would kick a poor old man. I shall leave this place. I was transformed from nothing that I see here.

He now travelled for a day or two longer, and then he came to a great black mountain, near the bottom of which was an opening like the mouth of a cave. This mountain, he had heard, was filled with caverns and underground passages, which were the abodes of dragons, evil spirits and horrid creatures of all kinds.

"Ah me!" said the Bee-man, with a sigh, "I suppose I ought to visit this place. If I am going to do this thing properly, I should look on all sides of the subject, and I may have been one of those dreadful creatures myself."

Thereupon he went to the mountain, and as he approached the opening of the passage which led into its inmost recesses, he saw, sitting upon the ground and leaning his back against a tree, a Languid Youth. "Good day," said this individual when he saw the Bee-man. "Are you going inside?"

"Yes," said the Bee-man, "that is what I intend to do."

"Then," said the Languid Youth, slowly rising to his feet, "I think I will go with you. I was told that if I went in there I should get my energies toned up, and they need it very much. But I did not feel equal to entering by myself, and I thought I would wait until someone came who was going in. I am very glad to see you, and we will enter together."

So the two went into the cave, and they had proceeded but a short distance when they met a very little creature, whom it was easy to recognize as a Very Imp. He was about two feet high and resembled in colour a freshly polished pair of boots. He was extremely lively and active, and came bounding towards them. "What did you two people come here for?" he asked.

"I came," said the Languid Youth, "to have my energies toned up."

"You have come to the right place," said the Very Imp. "We will tone you up. And what does that old Bee-man want?"

"He has been transformed from something, and wants to find out what it is. He thinks he may have been one of the things in here."

"I should not wonder if that were so," said the Very Imp, rolling his head on one side and eyeing the Bee-man with a critical gaze. "All right," continued the Very Imp, "he can go around and pick out his previous existence. We have here all sorts of vile creepers, crawlers, hissers and snorters. I suppose he thinks anything will be better than a Bee-man."

"It is not because I want to be better than I am," said the Bee-man, "that I started out on this search. I have simply an honest desire to become what I originally was."

"Oh! That is it, is it?" said the other. "There is an idiotic mooncalf here, with a clam head, which must be very much like what you used to be."

"Nonsense," said the Bee-man. "You have not the least idea what an honest purpose is. I shall go about and see for myself."

"Go on," said the Very Imp, "and I will attend to this fellow who wants to be toned up." So saying, he joined the Languid Youth.

"Look here," said that individual, regarding him with interest, "do you black and shine yourself every morning?" "No," said the other, "it is waterproof varnish. You want to be invigorated, don't you? Well, I will tell you a splendid way to begin. You see that Bee-man has put down his hive and his coat with the bees in it. Just wait till he gets out of sight, and then catch a lot of those

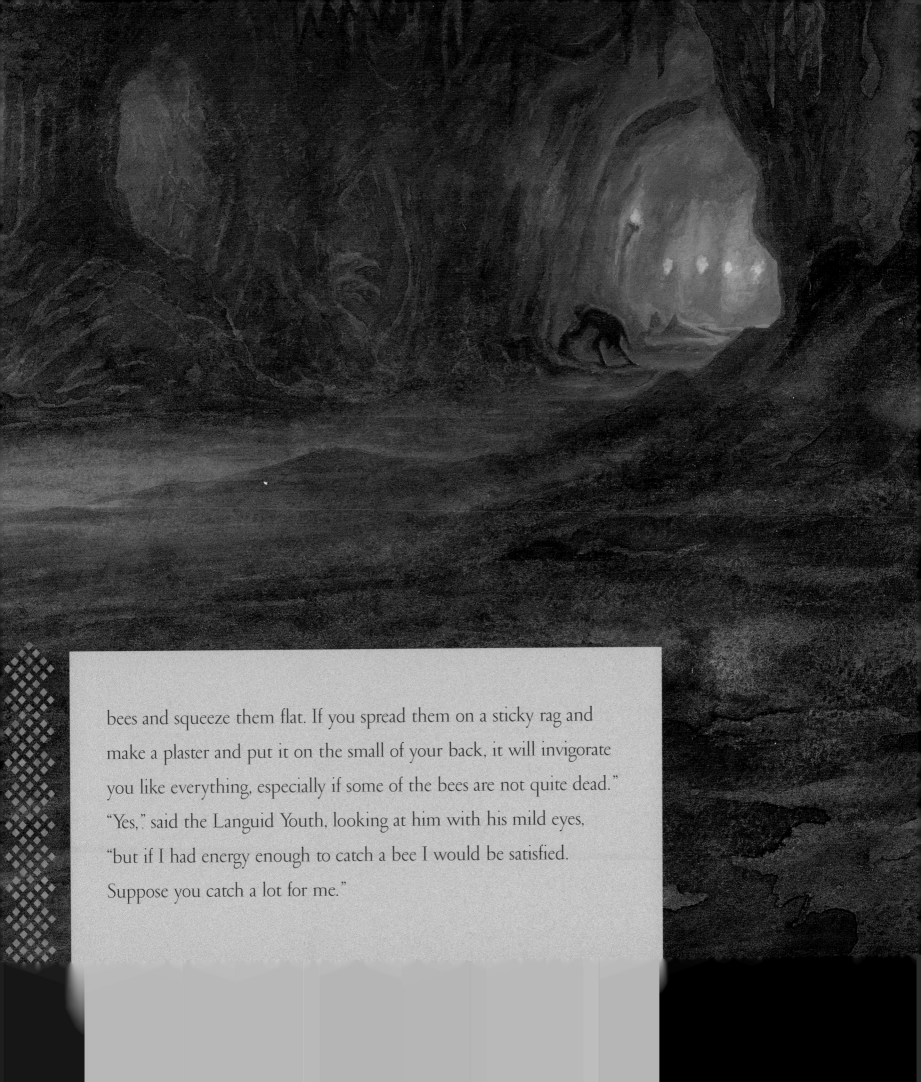

bees and squeeze them flat. If you spread them on a sticky rag and make a plaster and put it on the small of your back, it will invigorate you like everything, especially if some of the bees are not quite dead." "Yes," said the Languid Youth, looking at him with his mild eyes, "but if I had energy enough to catch a bee I would be satisfied. Suppose you catch a lot for me."

"The subject is changed," said the Very Imp. "We are now about to visit the spacious chamber of the King of the Snapdragons."

"That is a flower," said the Languid Youth.

"You will find him a gay old blossom," said the other. "When he has chased you round his room, and has blown sparks at you, and has snorted and howled and cracked his tail and snapped his jaws like a pair of anvils, your energies will be toned up higher than ever before in your life."

"No doubt of it," said the Languid Youth. "But I think I will begin with something a little milder."

"Well then," said the other, "there is a flat-tailed Demon of the Gorge in here. He is generally asleep, and, if you say so, you can slip into the farthest corner of his cave and I'll solder his tail to the opposite wall. Then he will rage and roar, but he can't get at you, for he doesn't reach all the way across his cave; I have measured him. It will tone you up wonderfully to sit there and watch him."

"Very likely," said the Languid Youth. "But I would rather stay outside and let you go up in the corner. The performance in that way will be more interesting to me."

"You are dreadfully hard to please," said the Very Imp. "I have offered them to you loose and I have offered them fastened to a wall, and now the best thing I can do is to give you a chance at one of them that can't move at all.

It is the Ghastly Griffin, and is enchanted. He can't stir so much as the tip of his whiskers for a thousand years. You can go to his cave and examine him just as if he were stuffed, and then you can sit on his back and think how it would be if you should live to be a thousand years old and he should wake up while you are sitting there. It would be easy to imagine a lot of horrible things he would do to you when you look at his open mouth with its awful fangs, his dreadful claws and his horrible wings all covered with spikes."

"I think that might suit me," said the Languid Youth. "I would much rather imagine the exercises of these monsters than to see them really going on."

"Come on, then," said the Very Imp, and he led the way to the cave of the Ghastly Griffin.

The Bee-man went by himself through a great part of the mountain and looked into many of its gloomy caves and recesses, recoiling in horror from most of the dreadful monsters who met his eyes.

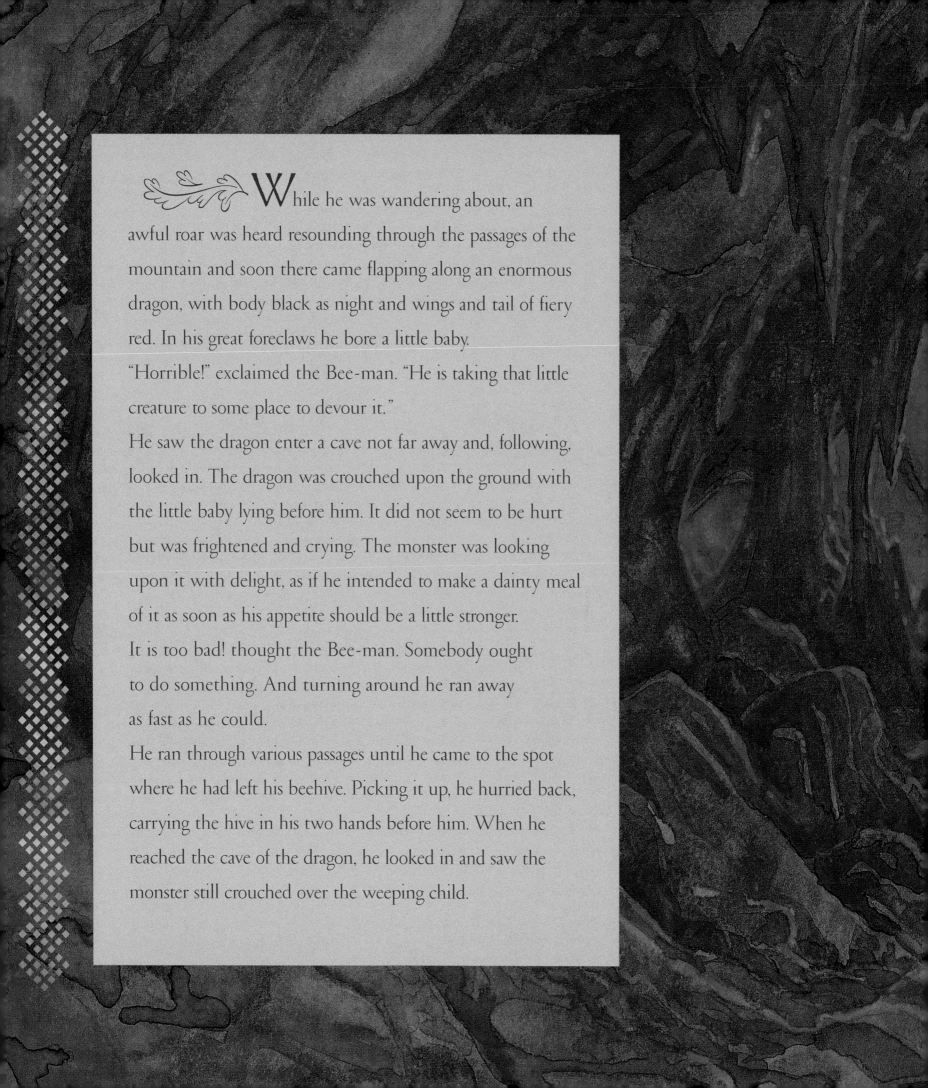

While he was wandering about, an awful roar was heard resounding through the passages of the mountain and soon there came flapping along an enormous dragon, with body black as night and wings and tail of fiery red. In his great foreclaws he bore a little baby.

"Horrible!" exclaimed the Bee-man. "He is taking that little creature to some place to devour it."

He saw the dragon enter a cave not far away and, following, looked in. The dragon was crouched upon the ground with the little baby lying before him. It did not seem to be hurt but was frightened and crying. The monster was looking upon it with delight, as if he intended to make a dainty meal of it as soon as his appetite should be a little stronger.

It is too bad! thought the Bee-man. Somebody ought to do something. And turning around he ran away as fast as he could.

He ran through various passages until he came to the spot where he had left his beehive. Picking it up, he hurried back, carrying the hive in his two hands before him. When he reached the cave of the dragon, he looked in and saw the monster still crouched over the weeping child.

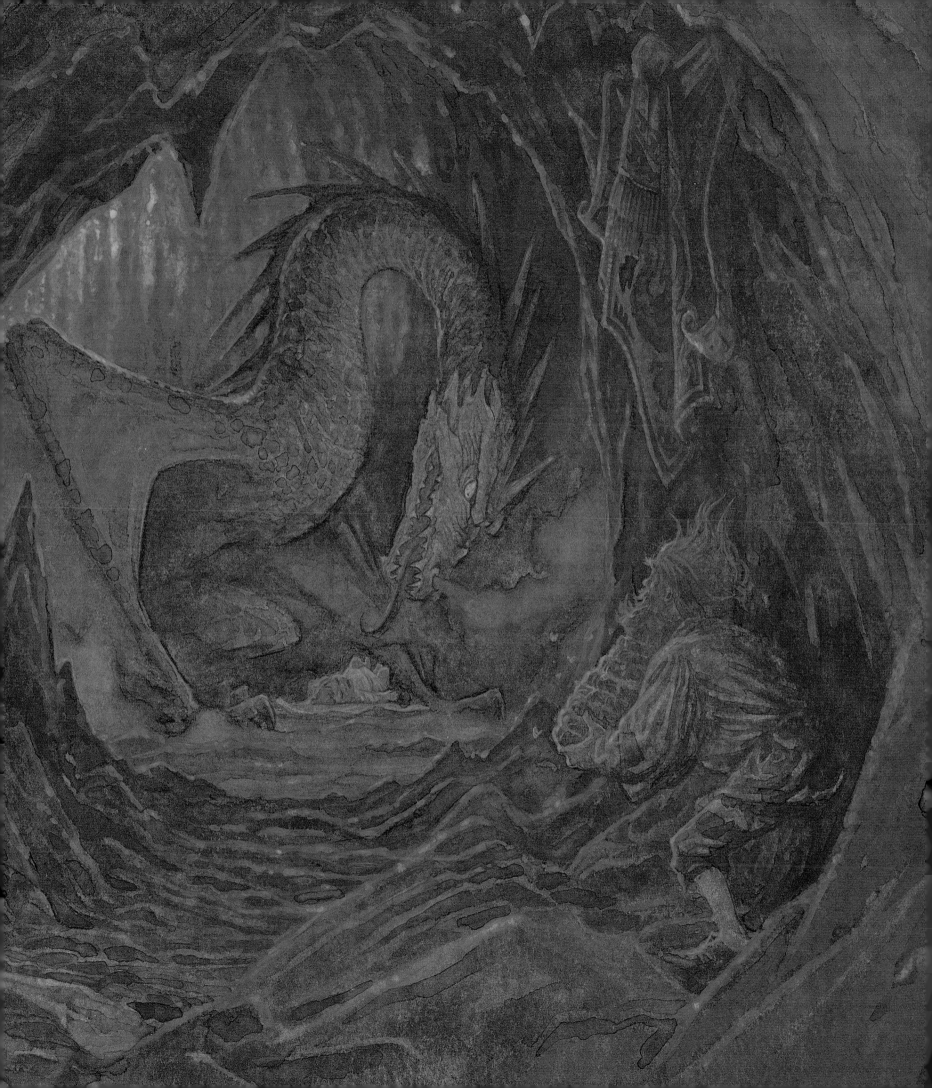

Without a moment's hesitation, the Bee-man rushed into the cave and threw his hive straight into the face of the dragon. The bees, enraged by the shock, rushed out in an angry crowd and immediately fell upon the head, mouth, eyes and nose of the dragon. The great monster, astounded by this sudden attack and driven almost wild by the numberless stings of the bees, sprang back to the farthest portion of his cave, still followed by his relentless enemies, at whom he flapped wildly with his great wings and struck with his paws.

While the dragon was thus engaged with the bees, the Bee-man rushed forward, seized the child and hurried away. He did not stop to pick up his doublet, but kept on until he reached the entrance of the caves.

There he saw the Very Imp, hopping along on one leg and rubbing his back and shoulders with his hands; he stopped to enquire what was the matter, and what had become of the Languid Youth.

"He is no kind of a fellow," said the Very Imp. "He disappointed me dreadfully.

I took him up to the Ghastly Griffin, and told him the thing was enchanted, and that he might sit on its back and think about what it could do if it were awake. But when he came near it the wretched creature opened its eyes and raised its head, and then you ought to have seen how mad that simpleton was. He made a dash at me and seized me by the ears. He kicked and beat me till I can scarcely move."

"His energies must have been toned up a good deal," said the Bee-man.

"Toned up! I should say so!" cried the other. "I raised a howl, and a Scissor-jawed Clipper came out of his hole and got after him. But that lazy fool ran so fast he could not be caught."

The Bee-man now ran on, and soon overtook the Languid Youth. "You need not be in a hurry now," said the latter, "for the rules of this institution don't allow the creatures inside to come out of this opening, or to hang around it. If they did, they would frighten away visitors. They go in and out of holes in the upper part of the mountain." The two proceeded on their way.

"What are you going to do with that baby?" said the Languid Youth.

"I shall carry it along with me as I go on with my search," said the Bee-man, "and perhaps I may find its mother. If I do not, I shall give it to somebody in the little village yonder. Anything would be better than leaving it to be devoured by that horrid dragon."

"Let me carry it. I feel quite strong enough now to carry a baby."

"Thank you," said the Bee-man, "but I can take it myself. I like to carry something, and I have now neither my hive nor my doublet."

"It is very well that you had to leave them behind," said the Youth, "for the bees would have stung the baby."

"My bees never sting babies," said the other.

"They probably never had a chance," remarked his companion.

They soon entered the village, and after walking a short distance the Youth exclaimed, "Do you see that woman over there, sitting at the door of her house? She has beautiful hair, and she is tearing it all to pieces. She should not be allowed to do that."

"No," said the Bee-man. "Her friends should tie her hands."

"Perhaps she is the mother of this child," said the Youth, "and if you give it to her she will no longer think of tearing her hair."

"But," said the Bee-man, "you don't really think this is her child?"

"Suppose you go over and see," said the other.

The Bee-man hesitated a moment, and then he walked towards the woman. Hearing him coming, she raised her head, and when she saw the child she rushed towards it, snatched it into her arms and, screaming with joy, she covered it with kisses. Then with happy tears she begged to know the story of the rescue of her child, whom she never expected to see again. She loaded the Bee-man with thanks and blessings, the friends and neighbours gathered around and there was great rejoicing.

The mother urged the Bee-man and the Youth to stay with her and rest and refresh themselves, which they were glad to do, as they were tired and hungry.

They remained at the cottage all night, and in the afternoon of the next day the Bee-man said to the Youth, "It may seem an odd thing to you, but never in all my life have I felt myself drawn towards any living being as I am drawn towards this baby. Therefore I believe that I have been transformed from a baby."

"Good!" cried the Youth. "It is my opinion that you have hit the truth. And would you really like to be changed back to your original form?"

"Indeed I would!" said the Bee-man. "I have the strongest yearning to be what I originally was."

The Youth, who had now lost every trace of languid feeling, took a great interest in the matter, and early the next morning started off to inform the Junior Sorcerer that the Bee-man had discovered what he had been transformed from, and desired to be changed back to it.

The Junior Sorcerer and his learned masters were filled with enthusiasm when they heard this report, and they at once set out for the mother's cottage, where, by magic arts, the Bee-man was changed  back into a baby. The mother was so grateful for what the Bee-man had done for her that she agreed to take charge of this baby and to bring it up with her own.

"It will be a grand thing for him," said the Junior Sorcerer, "and I am glad I studied his case. He will now have a fresh start in life, and will have a chance to become something better than a miserable old man living in a wretched hut, with no friends or companions but buzzing bees."

The Junior Sorcerer and his masters then returned to their homes, happy in the success of their great performance. And the Youth went back to his home anxious to begin a life of activity and energy.

Years and years afterwards, when the Junior Sorcerer had become a Senior and was very old indeed, he passed through the country of Orn and noticed a small hut about which swarms of bees were flying.

He approached it, and looking in at the door he saw an old man in a leather doublet, sitting at a table, eating honey. By his magic art he knew this was the baby which had been transformed from the Bee-man.

"Upon my word!" exclaimed the Sorcerer, "he has grown into the same thing again!"

This edition first published 2003 by Walker Books Ltd
87 Vauxhall Walk, London SE11 5HJ

2 4 6 8 10 9 7 5 3 1

Illustrations © 2003 P. J. Lynch

The right of P. J. Lynch to be identified as the illustrator of this work has been asserted
by him in accordance with the Copyright, Designs and Patents Act 1988

This book has been typeset in Garamond Ludlow with Galahad titling

Printed in Italy

British Library Cataloguing in Publication Data:
a catalogue record for this book is available from the British Library

ISBN 0-7445-9612-2

www.walkerbooks.co.uk